M000042029

THE SWEET NELLIE
NOSTALGIA GIFT BOOKS

With Thanks & Appreciation
The Pleasure of Your Company
With Love & Affection
Motherly Devotion
I Thee Wed
A Christmas Gathering
One Swell Dad
Baby Dear
A Birthday Wish

The Grandest Folks

To ______________________________

From ____________________________

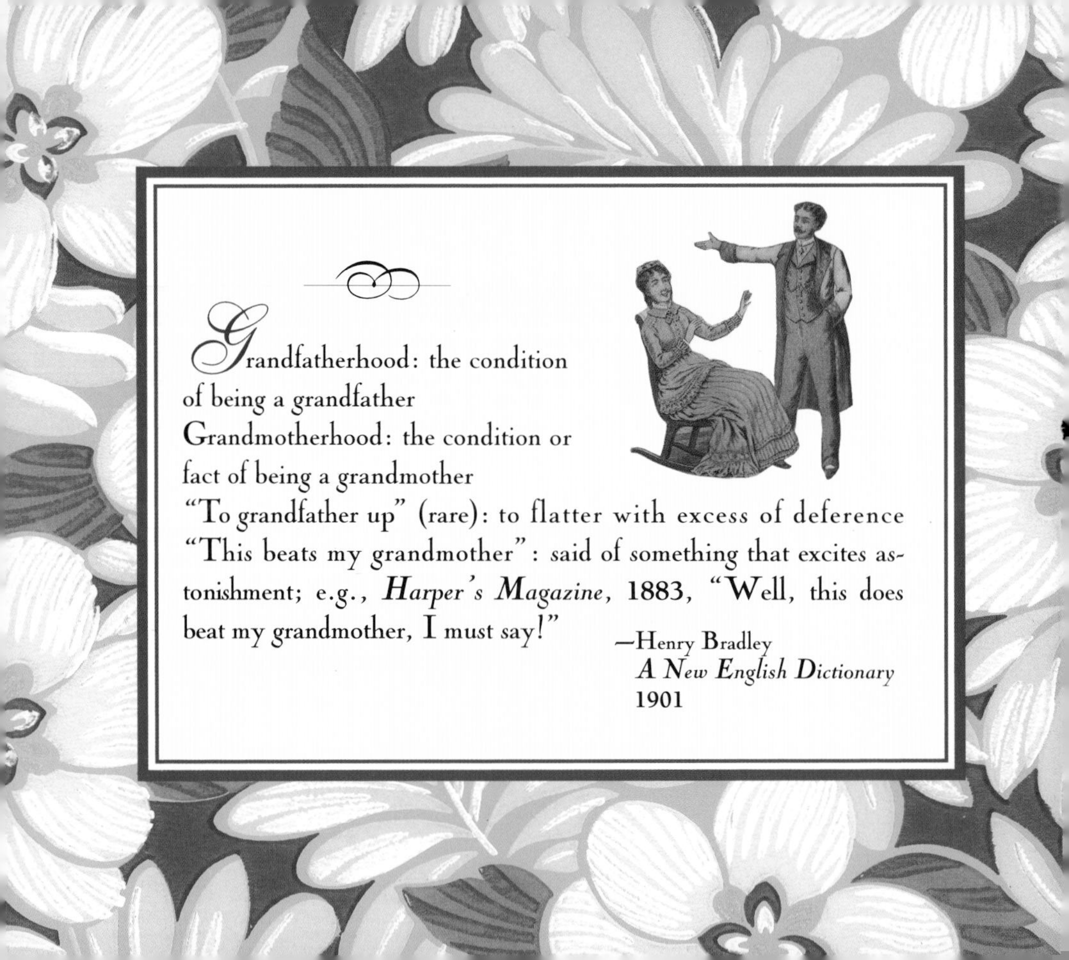

Grandfatherhood: the condition of being a grandfather
Grandmotherhood: the condition or fact of being a grandmother
"To grandfather up" (rare): to flatter with excess of deference
"This beats my grandmother" : said of something that excites astonishment; e.g., *Harper's Magazine*, 1883, "Well, this does beat my grandmother, I must say!"

—Henry Bradley
A New English Dictionary
1901

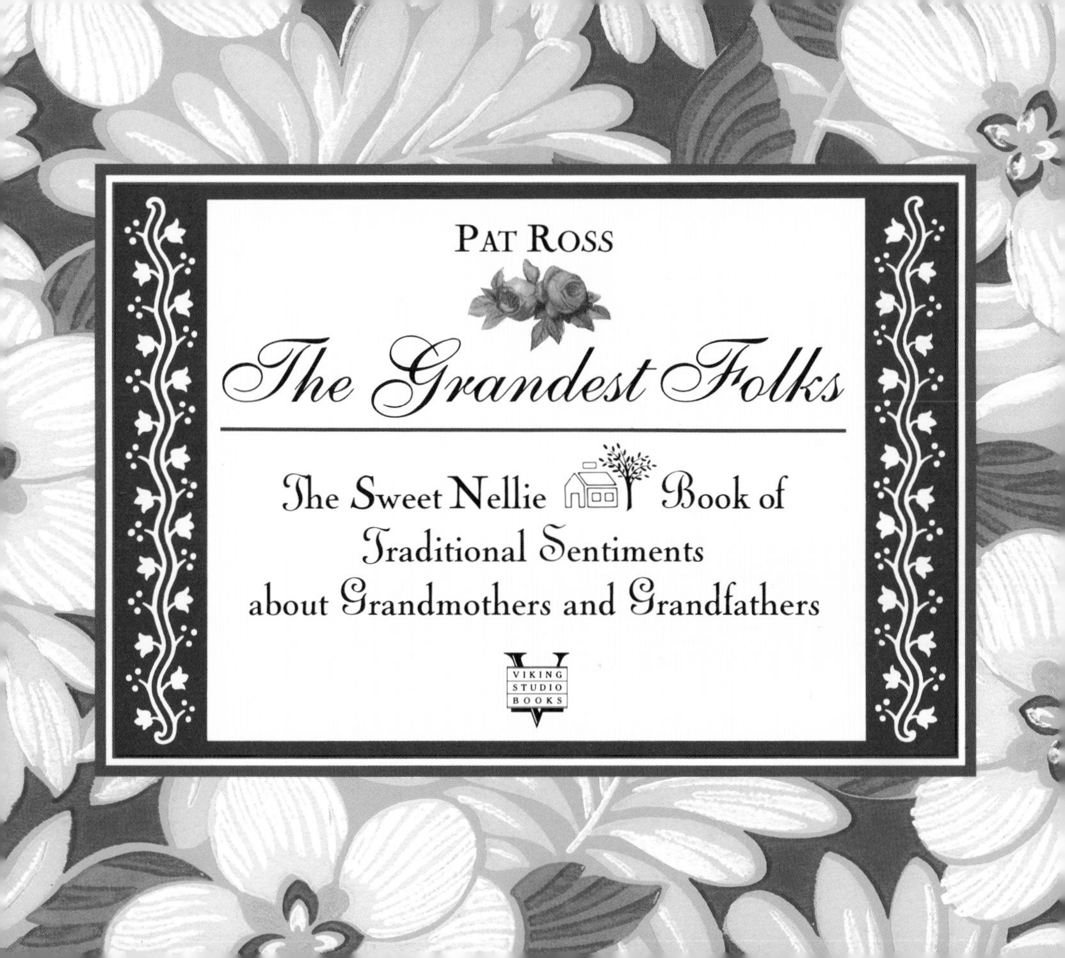

PAT ROSS

The Grandest Folks

The Sweet Nellie Book of Traditional Sentiments about Grandmothers and Grandfathers

VIKING STUDIO BOOKS

VIKING STUDIO BOOKS
Published by the Penguin Group
Penguin Books USA Inc., 375 Hudson Street, New York, New York 10014, U.S.A.
Penguin Books Ltd, 27 Wrights Lane, London W8 5TZ, England
Penguin Books Australia Ltd, Ringwood, Victoria, Australia
Penguin Books Canada Ltd, 10 Alcorn Avenue,
Toronto, Ontario, Canada M4V 3B2
Penguin Books (N.Z.) Ltd, 182-190 Wairau Road, Auckland 10, New Zealand

Penguin Books Ltd, Registered Offices: Harmondsworth, Middlesex, England

First published in 1993 by Viking Penguin,
a division of Penguin Books USA Inc.

1 3 5 7 9 10 8 6 4 2

ISBN 0-670-84731-3
CIP data available

Printed in Japan
Set in Nicholas Cochin
Designed by Virginia Norey and Amy Hill

INTRODUCTION

How fortunate we are today to have grandparents—and great-grandparents—who are young enough in both years and spirit to influence our lives. Nineteenth-century families occasionally boasted a revered septuagenarian, though our image is of someone bent and bespectacled, sweetly dotty or thoroughly crusty. Today grandparents of the same age run marathons and dance till midnight! But past or present, they have a special connection to the generation that calls them Grandma and Grandpa, Nanny and Pop-pop, Grams and Gramps, or the plentiful fond variations, and treasurestheir company.

My maternal grandparents drove a black De Soto. During the fifties, it was a most solid and respectable sort of car. Occasionally, the year of the car would change, but that conventional car always seemed

the same to me. When Nanny and Pop took me for a Sunday ride, the durable upholstery scratched my bare legs, but the springy ride across country roads was better than any roller coaster. The center of attention, I was their princess in the big backseat, and I behaved accordingly. When I slept over, the sheets at my grandparents' felt cooler, their mattress softer, their lavender-scented towels thicker. There was no air-conditioning then, yet their house—tightly shuttered on sweltering Baltimore days—remained cool.

When Pop finally came home with their first TV, Nanny found a place for it—in a corner behind a tall wing chair! It was not her idea of progress. We all huddled together for a "show" turned so low–in deference to Nanny, of course–that we learned to read lips. They stopped manufacturing the De Soto in the late fifties, but my grandparents never bought another car. Instead, a second car, the "salvage" car, sat on blocks in their garage, lending spare parts to its twin till my grandfather could no longer drive.

I am lucky to have these stories to tell, these memories to share. The relationship between grandparents and grandchildren is often less complicated and, therefore, more joyful than that between parents and children. It is no wonder that literature speaks so warmly of the special connections that exist between "the grandest folks" and the generation who appreciates them the most. This small volume helps to celebrate their presence in our lives.

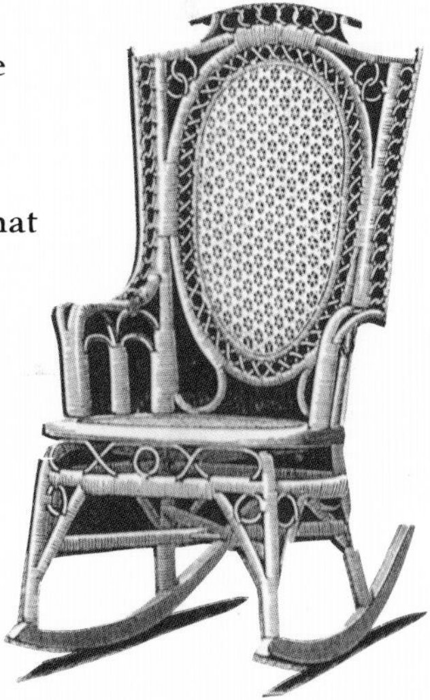

Presented by Herrick & Lodewick,
328 Broadway, SARATOGA, N. Y.
EDWIN C. BURT.
FINE SHOES

Small Pride

The case of a first grandchild is more like the conferring of a decoration or order (Order of the Bath, perhaps), and one is inclined to sit ostentatiously on a twig and preen one's feathers. It's funny—just plain funny—to see your own baby with a baby of her own.

—Mrs. Clipston Sturgis
Random Reflections of a Grandmother
1917

I always wondered how the fact would feel—
To be a grandfather! Oh, other men
Had boasted of it—but I scarce believed
That they were truly thrilled with hope again.
But now I, too, with Little Fellow there
Feel strong, renewed—as if my hands, which, numb,
Clung futilely to Life had gained fresh grasp.
I've laid a lien on ages still to come!

—Theodora Bates Cogswell
"The Grandfather"
1939

LYDIA E. PINKHAM'S
Grandchildren.

My brain reels in a dizzy whirl of pronouns, but my doubts are at an end, and my questions answered: Occupation? GRANDMOTHER.

—Mrs. Clipston Sturgis
Random Reflections of a Grandmother
1917

Grandmother was sitting in a low rocking-chair, with the baby in her arms, bending over it with eyes of worship.

—Laura E. Richards
Grandmother
1907

It begins when the first baby is expected, and you think you are all in all necessary to the occasion only to find out that you are neither wanted nor expected; and then receive a hurry call at the last minute to say that after all you had better come.

—Mrs. Clipston Sturgis
Random Reflections of a Grandmother
1917

The children born with golden spoons usually had grandparents born with iron spoons in their mouths. A little iron in the blood is a tremendously good thing.

—Margaret E. Sangster
Good Manners for All Occasions
1905

With the coming of that little creature the world changed once again for Grandmother.

—Laura E. Richards
Grandmother
1907

Memories of
Grandmother

My grandmother often lectured me and others on our waste of time because we would read while tending baby brothers and sisters, boasting that her time was better employed: "When I used to tend my brother I used to put him down between my feet, giving him playthings, and so then I could go on with my sewing." I had many a cry about it, but my mother, having been better taught, always took my part, so that at length, Grandma concluded to leave us to our own ways, and no doubt trembled for the industry of the rising generation.

—Mary (Palmer) Tyler
Grandmother Tyler's Book
1925

My picture of contentment: The chimes were ringing in the church tower. I was peeling potatoes while a pie cooled on the windowsill. Grandma was upstairs listening to her favorite radio story as she mended the overalls. One boy sat on the kitchen floor licking the baking pans and another was in the yard while his Daddy showed him how to use a fly rod. The dog slept in a square of sunlight on the porch. God's in His heaven, all's right with the world.

—Katherine Piper
Herald-Ledger of Eldora, Iowa
1952

We . . . ventured to express our curiosity respecting the contents of various trunks, parcels, and curious-looking boxes. My grandmother indulged our curiosity to the utmost. . . . Now a rich brocaded petticoat called up phantoms of the past, when ladies wore high-heeled shoes, and waists of no size at all . . . and gentlemen felt magnificently attired in powdered curls and cues, and as many ruffles would fill a modern dressing gown.

—Ella Rodman (Church)
A Grandmother's Recollections
1851

Quite early almost every woman in North Stonefield had got herself an eggbeater, and a great many were buying sewing machines. Grandma would have none of such devices. When, later, the automobile came along, Grandma always tried to stand in the way of it, literally and figuratively.

—Bertha Damon
Grandma Called It Carnal
1938

She loved her housework, and did it with a pretty grace and quickness; she loved to sit by Grandfather with her sewing, or read the paper to him.

—Laura E. Richards
Grandmother
1907

Her opinions are not many, not new. She thinks the young women of the present day too forward, and the men not respectful enough: but hopes her grandchildren will be better; though she differs with her daughter in several points respecting their management.

—William Hone
The Every-day Book
1827

Although my grandmother could so easily assume a stern and commanding air, it was by no means habitual to her; and the children, though they feared and never dared to dispute her authority, soon loved her with all the pure, unselfish love of childhood, which cannot be bought.

—Ella Rodman (Church)
A Grandmother's Recollections
1851

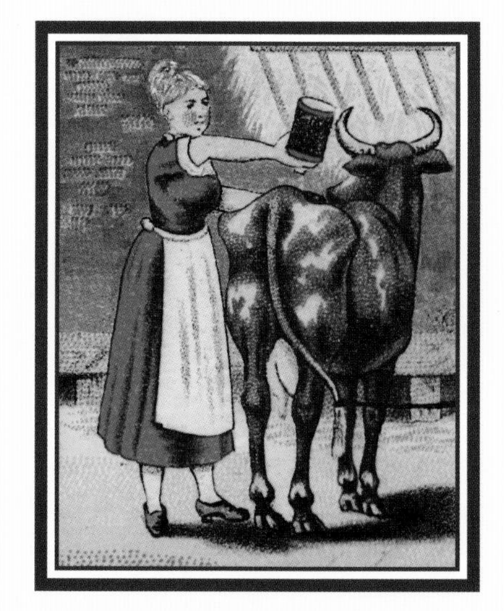

Grandma's manner, though I cannot imagine where in her environment she could have found example, was dignified yet gracious; even when she was brushing the hearth or leading Juno the cow around the flower bed she somehow looked distinguished.

—Bertha Damon
Grandma Called It Carnal
1938

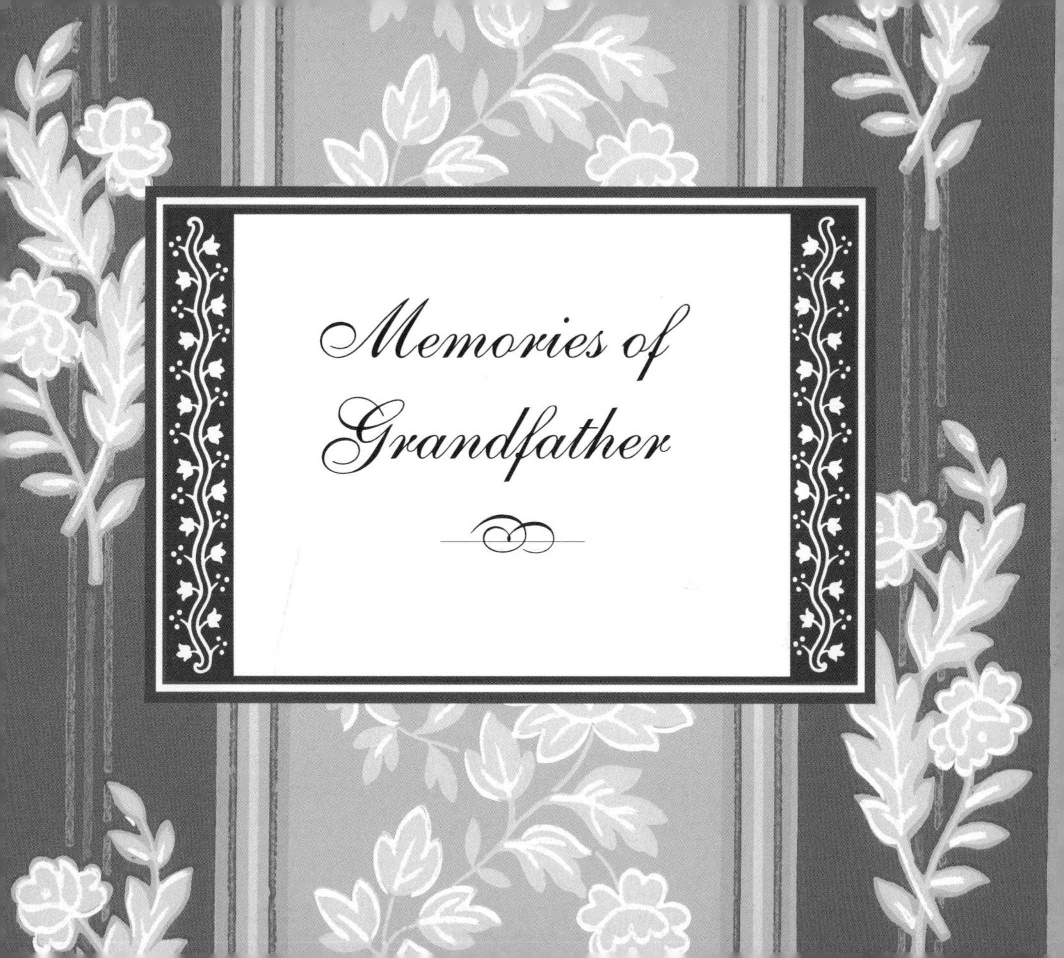
Memories of
Grandfather

Over the river and through the wood,
To grandfather's house we go . . .
The horse knows the way
To carry the sleigh
Through the white and drifted snow.

Over the river and through the wood–
Now grandmother's cap I spy!
Hurrah for the fun!
Is the pudding done?
Hurrah for the pumpkin pie!

–Lydia Maria Child
"Thanksgiving Day"
c. 1870

My early recollection is of a patriarchally bearded and imposing figure in a Boston rocker beside a Franklin stove. From the ample expanse of beard issued a calm and preceptorial voice, dispensing admonition, instruction, exhortation to be good and warning against evil conduct, sage advice and stern reproof.

—Samuel Hopkins Adams
Grandfather Stories
1955

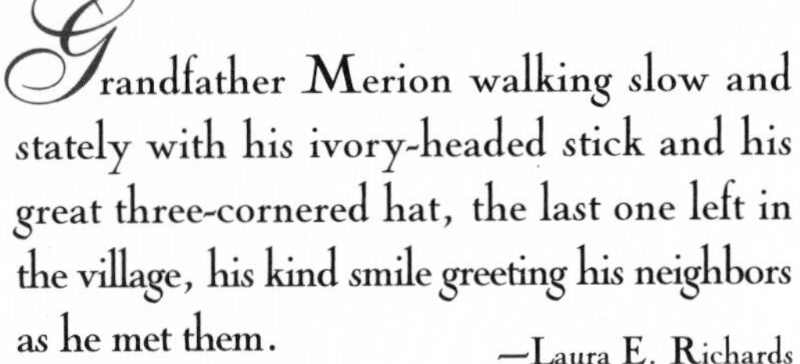

Grandfather Merion walking slow and stately with his ivory-headed stick and his great three-cornered hat, the last one left in the village, his kind smile greeting his neighbors as he met them.

—Laura E. Richards
Grandmother
1907

My grandfather, Gregory Shanahan, the eldest child, remembered, when a little child, of sitting on the floor and playing with his grandpa Shonan's silver buckles on his slippers.

—Grandma Moses
My Life's History
1948

Sometimes Grandpa used to hum some of the church songs when he was sitting in his rocking chair out on the porch patting his foot and watching the sun go down behind Mr. Hayward's tobacco barn.

—Claude Brown
Manchild in the Promised Land
1965

The only one in the house who wasn't afraid of grandfather was my small and peppery grandmother with the corners of her silk headkerchief always fluttering under her chin.

—Isaac Bashevis Singer
Of a World That Is No More
1970

At my grandfather's house at noontime we had soup and two or three kinds of meat, fried chicken, fried ham, or spareribs or liver pudding; and we had four or five vegetables and a dessert or so and fruit.

—Ben Robertson
Red Hills and Cotton
1942

Words of Wisdom

Surely, two of the most satisfying experiences in life must be those of being a grandchild or a grandparent.

—Donald A. Norberg
Monroe County News of Albia, Iowa
1952

My grandmother took occasion to give me some very good advice with respect to the behavior of hardly-grown girls; she remarked that they should be careful not to engross the conversation, and also, that quiet people were always more interesting than loud talkers.

—Ella Rodman (Church)
A Grandmother's Recollections
1851

Grandparents have a toleration for and patience with the boys and girls that parents lack.

—Margaret E. Sangster
Good Manners for All Occasions
1905

In grandmother's day, if she dropped a fork while doing the dishes it was a sign she was going to have callers.

—Tom Kelly
Reporter of Emmetsburg, Iowa
1952

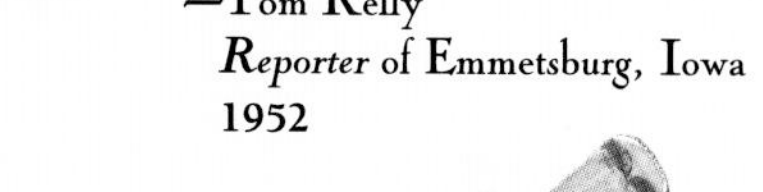

My grandmother said cabbage boiled less than four hours would kill you.

—Ben Robertson
Red Hills and Cotton
1942

Be virtuous; govern your passions; retain your appetites; avoid excess and high-seasoned foods; eat slowly, and chew your food well. Do not eat to full satiety. Breakfast betimes; it is not healthy to go out fasting. In winter, a glass of wine is an excellent preservative against unwholesome air. . . . Avoid salted meats: those who eat them often have pale complexions, a slow pulse, and are full of corrupted humors.

—William Hone
The Every-day Book
1827

If you know the father and grandfather you may trust the son.

—Moroccan proverb

Every generation revolts against its fathers and makes friends with its grandfathers.

—Lewis Mumford
The Brown Decades
1931

Old Folks' Party,
WEDNESDAY, Aug. 23.
BROCKTON BAND.

Once Removed

"But were you ever young, grandmother? I mean," she continued, a little frightened at her own temerity, "were you ever as little as I am now?"

—Ella Rodman (Church)
A Grandmother's Recollections
1851

Even now I am not old, I never think of it, yet I am a grandmother to 11 grandchildren, I also have 17 great-grandchildren, that's plenty!

—Grandma Moses
My Life's History
1948

Then grandma lifted her darling,
And patted his head on her breast,
And sang in a tremulous treble,
Till all Bobby's woes were at rest.
And so the wee whip, bright and yellow,
Was laid on the mantel again—
And that is the way that the grandmas
Spoil nine little boys out of ten.

—May Riley Smith
"Our Bobby Was Pinching the Kitten"
1893

Grandfather clock: A large clock intended to be placed against a wall, especially one with a tall case enclosing a long pendulum and weights, made from shortly after the invention of the pendulum in 1656, first in England and then throughout Europe and North America.

—*Penguin Dictionary of Decorative Arts*
Viking
c. 1977, 1989

This is Ba-by's first jour-ney. She sits up in the car seat as straight as mam-ma. She is go-ing to grand-pa's house. With her own mon-ey she has bought some ro-ses to car-ry to grand-ma.
Won't grand-ma think the ba-by sweet?

—*Baby's Journey and Other Stories*

Was there ever a grandparent, bushed after a day of minding noisy youngsters, who hasn't felt the Lord knew what He was doing when He gave little children to young people?

—Joe E. Wells
Courier of Coloma, Michigan
1952

One of the last dances was an old-fashioned country dance, called "the grandfather," when each couple in turn passed along holding a handkerchief, over which all the others had to jump.

—Henry Bradley
"Pall Mall Magazine"
August 1897

I anticipate with much pleasure sitting on a little pink cloud in the hereafter, and watching my granddaughter upsetting all her mother's most cherished convictions.

—Mrs. Clipston Sturgis
Random Reflections of a Grandmother
1917

I have ever had pleasure in obtaining any little anecdotes of my ancestors.

—Benjamin Franklin
Autobiography
1771

Young Hearts

There is frost on their heads and sunshine in their souls.

—Margaret E. Sangster
Good Manners for All Occasions
1905

My age is as a lusty Winter,
Frosty, but Kindly.

—William Shakespeare
As You Like It
1600

Nature is full of freaks, and now puts an old head on young shoulders, and then a young heart beating under fourscore winters.

—Ralph Waldo Emerson
Society and Solitude
1870

I am still learning.

—Michelangelo
(his motto)

One of the compensations for age is that you can brag about your youth with less likelihood of being contradicted.

—A. Monroe Courtright
Public Opinion of Westerville, Ohio
1952

Years, I am glad of them;
Would that I had of them
More and yet more, while thus mingled with thine
Age, I make light of it,
Fear not the sight of it,
Time's but our playmate, whose toys are divine.

—Thomas Wentworth Higginson
"Sixty and Six"
1889

There is no power in ancestry to make the foolish wise.

—Sarah Josepha Hale
Ormond Grosvenor
1835

You are beautiful and faded
Like an old opera tune
Played upon a harpsichord.

—Amy Lowell
"A Lady"
1914

I am long on ideas, but short on time. I expect to live to be about only a hundred.

—Thomas Edison
in *The Golden Book Magazine*
April 1931

I love to look on a scene like this,
Of wild and careless play,
And persuade myself that I am not old,
And my locks are not yet gray;
For it stirs the blood in an old man's heart,
And make his pulses fly,
To catch the thrill of a happy voice,
And the light of a pleasant eye.

—John Greenleaf Whittier
"Child Life"
1875

It seems fitting that a book about traditions of the past should be decorated with period artwork. In that spirit, the art in *The Grandest Folks* has been taken from personal collections of original nineteenth-century and early twentieth-century drawings, advertising cards, magazines, and other popular treasures of the time.

The endpapers and part-title pages show patterns reproduced from some of our favorite vintage wallpapers.

SEVENTY